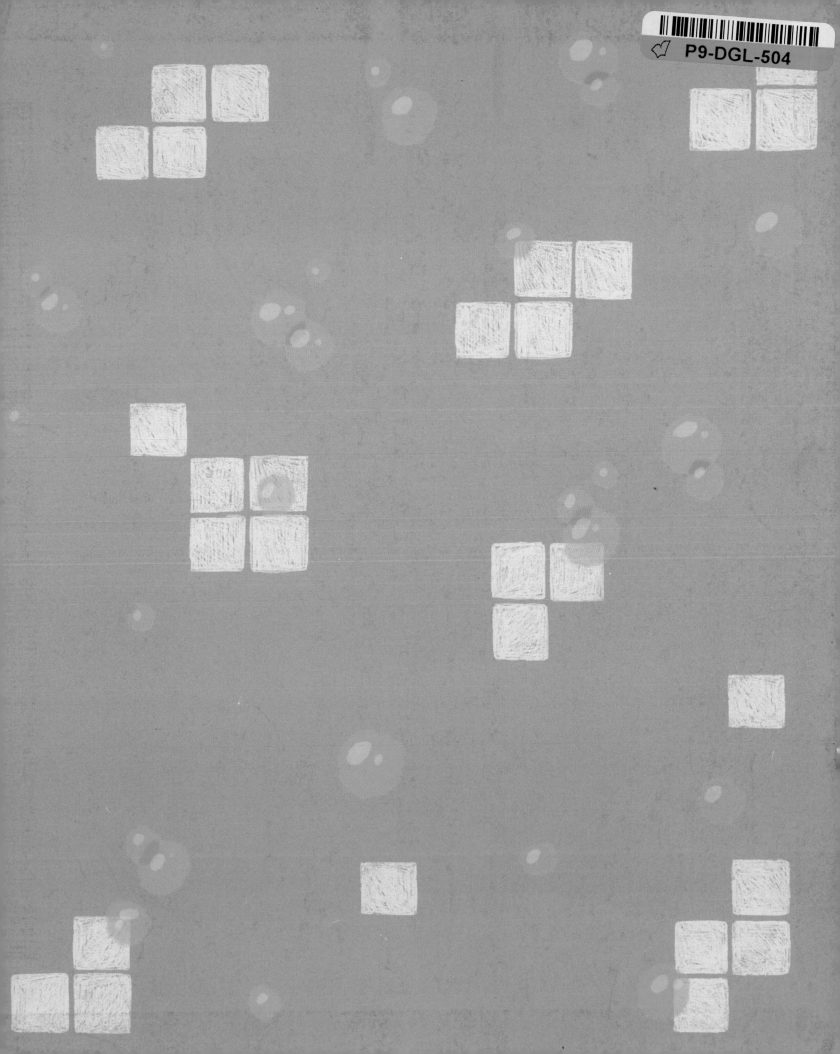

FOR MEALLA AND SOLA
–D.U.

FOR MY FAMILY
–M.H.

Dial Books for Young Readers
Penguin Young Readers Group
An imprint of Penguin Random House LLC
375 Hudson Street
New York, NY 10014

Printed in China
ISBN 9780803741010

1   3   5   7   9   10   8   6   4   2

Design by Jennifer Kelly
Text set in Skippy Sharp Custom and True North Black

The artwork for this book was created digitally.

WALRUS IN THE BATHTUB

BY
DEBORAH UNDERWOOD

ILLUSTRATED BY
MATT HUNT

DIAL
BOOKS
FOR YOUNG
READERS

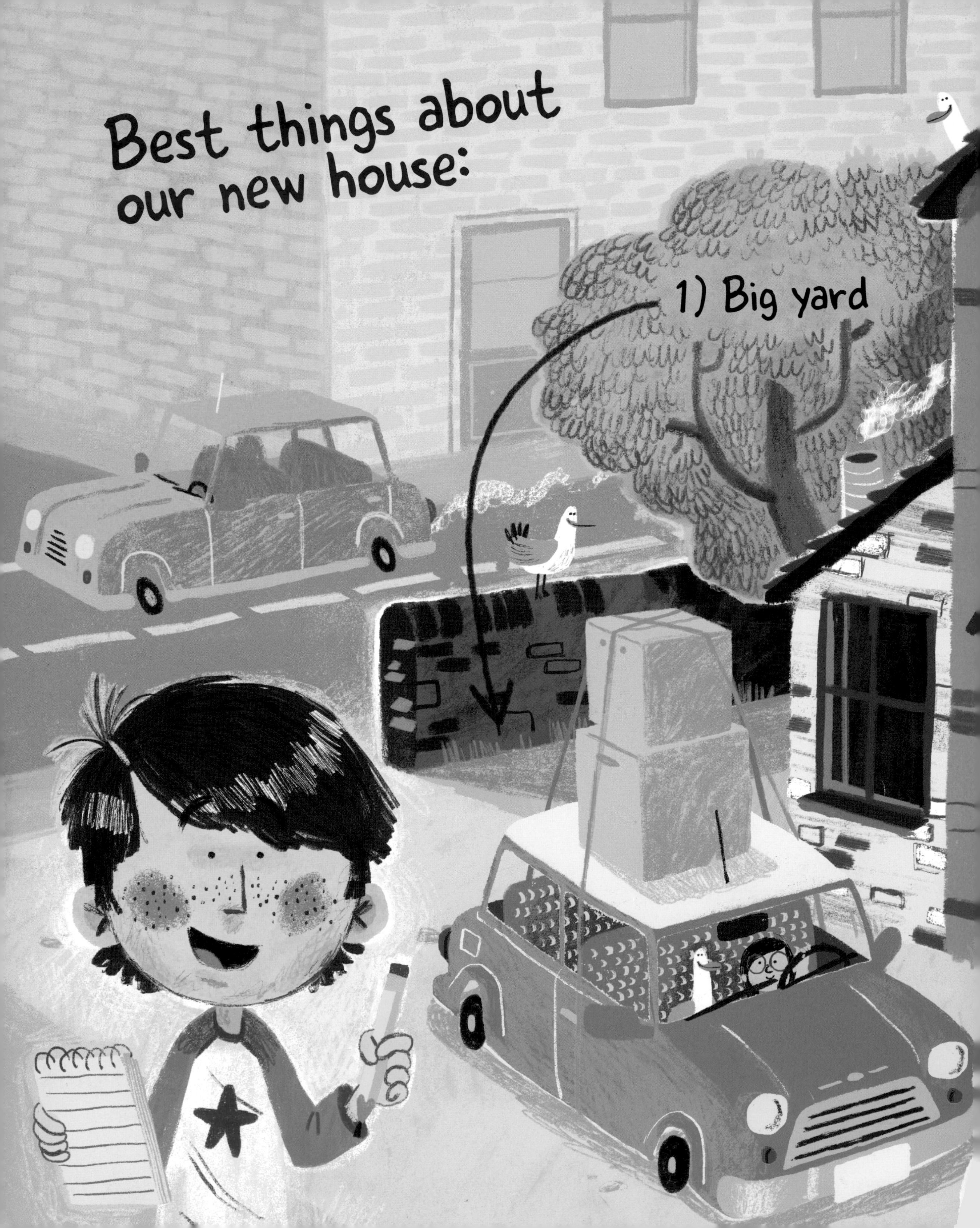
Best things about our new house:
1) Big yard

1) Walrus in the bathtub

Bad things about having a **walrus** in the bathtub:

1) Clam shells

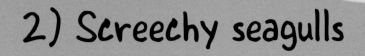

2) Screechy seagulls

3) Bathtub tidal waves

More bad things
about having a walrus in the bathtub:

1) Soggy suppers

2) Wet towels

3) Toothpaste troubles

WHO USED ALL THE TOOTHPASTE?

GUESS.

Ways to try to get a walrus out of the bathtub:

1) Have a clam giveaway

2) Dress up like a killer whale

RAWR!

3) Dress your dad up like a lady walrus

WELL, I THINK YOU'RE CUTE, DEAR.

WORST things about having a walrus in the bathtub:

1) Dial-a-Clam deliveries

3) Walrus songs

Reason we have to move again:

1) WALRUS!

WALRUS WEEKLY HOME EDITION
HOW TO MAKE YOUR NEW FAMILY FEEL WELCOME
1 ORDER IN FOOD
2 THROW THEM A PARTY
3 SING THEM A NICE LONG WALRUS SONG!

~~Bad~~ Great things about having a walrus in the bathtub:

1) ~~Clam shells~~ Free art supplies!

2) ~~Screechy seagulls~~ No wasted food!

3) ~~Bathtub tidal waves~~
Indoor puddle jumping!

How to make your walrus feel welcome:
1) Order in food
2) Throw him a party
3) Sing him a nice, long walrus song!

Best thing about our new house:

1) Walrus in the bathtub!